What do you get if you put two monkeys with two children? An embarrassing bus ride, a chaotic tea-party, some deafening piano playing, a terrific mud fight, and a case of mistaken identity. Poor Mr Mullins, the zoo keeper, simply can't keep up.

He could have done with some help from Thunder, the parrot and hero of the second story in this collection of two. Thunder brings David nothing but good luck during his visit – and all without once leaving his cage!

Mark Burgess is well-known as an illustrator of humorous children's books, with some twenty books published. He has also created more than four hundred greetings card designs. *Monkey Business* is based on a real event. Between graduating from Art School and taking up illustration full-time, Mark worked at London Zoo and actually saw a monkey escape from its cage and be lured back again by bananas! He got the idea for *Lucky Thunder* from a conversation he had with a small green parrot he met at a party.

Monkey Business

Mark Burgess

Illustrated by the author

PUFFIN BOOKS
in association with
Blackie and Son Limited

PUFFIN BOOKS

Published by the Penguin Group
Penguin Books Ltd, 27 Wrights Lane, London W8 5TZ, England
Viking Penguin, a division of Penguin Books USA Inc.
375 Hudson Street, New York, New York 10014, USA
Penguin Books Australia Ltd, Ringwood, Victoria, Australia
Penguin Books Canada Ltd, 2801 John Street, Markham, Ontario, Canada L3R 1B4
Penguin Books (NZ) Ltd, 182–190 Wairau Road, Auckland 10, New Zealand

Penguin Books Ltd, Registered Offices: Harmondsworth, Middlesex, England

Monkey Business first published in Blackie Bears by Blackie and Son Limited 1987
Lucky Thunder first published in Blackie Bears by Blackie and Son Limited 1989
Published in one volume in Puffin Books 1991
1 3 5 7 9 10 8 6 4 2

Printed in England by Clays Ltd, St Ives plc

Contents

Monkey Business

'Ouch!' said Mr Mullins.

Mr Mullins was the keeper in charge of the monkeys at the Zoo. One of the monkeys had just pulled his ear. 'Ow! Don't do that!' said Mr Mullins. 'Stop it at once!'

Another monkey stole his cap and ran off with it.

'Stop it! Stop it!' said Mr Mullins. 'Give that back AT ONCE!'

The monkeys thought this was great fun. So did Simon and Mary Smith who were watching. They were visiting the Zoo with their father. The monkey, who was called Jo-jo, gave Mr Mullins back his cap and then took his glasses. 'Oh! Help! Help!' shouted Mr Mullins.

Mr Mullins was helpless without his glasses. The world around him became a misty

blur. He had to walk about with his arms stretched out in front of him. And he bumped into things.

'Ow! Ouch! Ohhhh!' said Mr Mullins.

Mr Mullins tripped over a stone and flopped into an old lorry tyre which hung on the end of a rope from the roof of the cage. He was stuck. All he could do was fling his arms and legs about in the air while the tyre

swung gently backwards and forwards. It looked as if he was trying to swim. The monkeys thought this was very funny. They laughed and laughed. The people watching laughed as well; they all thought Mr Mullins was doing it on purpose.

At the other end of the cage two monkeys were playing with the door. Mr Mullins hadn't shut it properly that morning and they had just got it open. Nobody saw them—except Mary, that is.

'Look!' said Mary. 'The monkeys are escaping!'

'Quick!' said Simon. 'We must stop them!'

They ran as fast as they could
and tried to close the cage door.

'It's stuck!' said Mary. 'Now
they'll all escape!'

The two monkeys leapt out of
the cage and started running
about outside. It wasn't long
before the other monkeys
realized the door was open. One
after another they jumped out of
the cage and then there were
monkeys everywhere, laughing

13

and swinging from branch to branch through the trees.

'Help! Help!' said Mr Mullins.

Bill Trunkett, the keeper in charge of the elephants, saw what had happened and blew his whistle. The other keepers heard the whistle and came to help. Sam Crouch, who looked after the lions, went to get a large bunch of bananas from the storeroom. Bill Trunkett rescued Mr Mullins and Sally Bream (who looked after the aquarium) found his glasses. Then Sam Crouch came back with the bananas. He gave some each to Mr Mullins, Bill Trunkett, Sally Bream and to Tony Nash who

had just come from the crocodile
house. Then they went off round
the Zoo waving the bananas.

'What are they doing?' said
Simon.

'They're going to catch the
monkeys, of course!' said Mary.
'Look! They're coming down out
of the trees!'

15

The monkeys couldn't resist
the bananas. They jumped down
from the trees and ran after the
keepers. But the keepers were
clever! They didn't give the
bananas to the monkeys straight
away but walked slowly back
towards the monkey cage. When
they reached the cage they

threw the bananas inside. All the monkeys ran in after the bananas and Mr Mullins closed the door. This time he made quite sure it was shut.

'Thank you, thank you everyone,' said Mr Mullins. Then Bill Trunkett went back to the elephant house, Sam Crouch went back to the lions, Sally Bream went back to the aquarium and Tony Nash went back to the crocodiles. Mr Mullins was just mopping his brow when he saw Mr Blaize the Head Keeper coming towards him.

'Hello, Mullins!' said Mr Blaize. 'Everything all right?'

Mr Blaize didn't know the monkeys had just escaped.

'Y-y-y-yes, Mr Blaize,' said Mr Mullins. He was rather afraid of Mr Blaize. Mr Blaize saw the bananas.

'Don't give them too many bananas, Mullins. We don't want them going to sleep. The public likes to see monkeys leaping about enjoying themselves.'

'Y-y-y-yes, Mr Blaize,' said Mr Mullins, who had gone quite pale.

'Good show, Mullins!' said Mr Blaize and he walked off towards the elephant house.

Simon and Mary had been counting the monkeys.

'I make it twenty-two,' said Mary.

'No, I'm sure it's only twenty-one,' said Simon. The monkeys were difficult to count as they moved about a lot.

'Let's ask the keeper,' said Mary.

They went up to Mr Mullins.
'Excuse me,' said Mary. 'Can
you tell us how many monkeys
there are? My brother says there
are twenty-one but I think there
are twenty-two.'

Mr Mullins looked surprised.
'Well, there should be twenty-
four,' he said. He counted the

monkeys himself. 'Oh dear,' he said. 'There *are* only twenty-two. Jo-jo and So-so are missing!' Mr Mullins looked very worried. He was thinking about what Mr Blaize would say when he found out. He would probably put Mr Mullins in charge of the crocodiles. Mr Mullins trembled at the thought. He was even more afraid of the crocodiles than he was of Mr Blaize.

'Don't worry,' said Mary. 'We'll look out for them for you.'

'Thank you,' said Mr Mullins but he still looked worried.

Simon and Mary went on walking round the Zoo with

their dad. 'Let's go and see
the elephants,' said their
dad.

'Oh yes!' said Simon.

'Oh, Dad, can we have an ice
cream?' said Mary. They were
just passing a kiosk.

'All right,' said their dad.
'Wait here and I'll go and get
some.' He went and stood in the
queue.

Something caught Mary's eye.
It was brown and was moving
about in the bushes by the Zoo
gates. Jo-jo and So-so.

'Simon, look! It's the
monkeys!' said Mary.

'Quick!' said Simon. 'We
mustn't lose sight of them.'

Simon and Mary's dad was just buying the ice creams. He didn't see the children run off after the monkeys.

'They've gone out of the Zoo!' shouted Mary.

'We're not supposed to go off on our own,' said Simon.

'Come *on*!' said Mary.

Simon and Mary followed the monkeys out of the Zoo. Jo-jo and So-so were just jumping on to a bus that had stopped outside. Simon and Mary managed to hop on before the bus started.

'Where are they?' said Mary.

'I don't know,' said Simon. 'I can't see them anywhere. Perhaps they're hiding under a seat.'

There was no sign of the monkeys.

'Shouldn't we tell someone?' said Mary.

'We'll tell the conductor when he comes,' said Simon.

There was a large lady sitting in front of them. She had a big bag of shopping beside her and on top was a bunch of bananas. Mary saw a furry brown hand

appear from under the seat and grab the bananas. 'Simon!' she whispered. 'There they are, under that seat!'

Simon was just leaning forward to look when the lady turned round.

'Stop tickling my legs!' she said.

'I wasn't tickling your legs,' said Simon, surprised.

'You must have been,' said the lady. 'Who else would do it?'

'I didn't do it, honest!' said Simon.

'Actually,' said Mary, 'I think there's a monkey under your seat.'

The lady snorted. 'Monkeys indeed!' she said. '*You*'re the monkeys! I shall tell the conductor.' Then she glanced at her shopping. 'Somebody's taken my bananas! Conductor! CONDUCTOR!'

The conductor came down from the top deck. 'What's going on here?' he said and then he

slipped on a banana skin.
'Oooooaaahhh!' he said as he
landed on his bottom. Money
went everywhere and his ticket
machine clicked out a whole roll
of tickets. The bus driver
stopped the bus and ran round
to see what had happened.

'It's all their fault!' said the
large lady in a loud voice.

'It wasn't us!' said Simon and
Mary. 'It was the monkeys.'

'What's been happening?' said
the bus driver.

'These two,' said the lady, pointing at Simon and Mary. 'They've taken my bananas.'

'We haven't!' said Simon, who felt like crying. 'There are some monkeys on the bus. They escaped from the Zoo and we followed them. *They* took the bananas!'

'A likely story!' said the bus conductor, who had got up and was rubbing his bottom.

'Where are they then, these monkeys?' said the bus driver.

'Under that seat!' said Mary.

'What rubbish!' said the lady.

'They are!' said Simon. 'Have a look!'

Everybody looked under the

seat. 'Nothing!' said the lady.

'They've gone!' said Mary.

'You're just a couple of trouble-makers,' said the lady crossly.

'Well, I don't know what to

make of it,' said the bus conductor. 'Where are your tickets?'

'We haven't any,' said Simon. 'And we haven't any money.'

'We were following the monkeys!' said Mary.

'Monkeys, monkeys! There aren't any monkeys!' said the bus conductor. 'And I'm sorry but if you haven't any tickets you can't travel on the bus. You'll have to get off.'

'I should think so!' said the lady. 'And good riddance!'

Simon and Mary got off the bus.

'Nobody believed us,' said Simon. 'What are we going to

do now? We've lost the monkeys
and Dad will be cross that we
ran off.'

'Let's walk to Granny's,' said
Mary. 'It's not far from here.'

'All right,' said Simon.

So that is what they did. As
they walked along they looked
for the monkeys. Simon found a
banana skin and once Mary
thought she heard monkeys
giggling behind a bush but there
was no one there. Jo-jo and
So-so had disappeared.

Just as they reached the road where Granny lived it began to rain. It wasn't just drizzle but hard, wetting rain. Simon and Mary ran as fast as they could to Granny's front door and rang the doorbell. Granny opened the door.

'Hello, Granny!' said Simon and Mary.

'Oh, hello, my dears!' said Granny. 'Come in quickly out of the rain. Where's Daddy?'

'He's at the Zoo, Granny,' said Mary. 'We left him there when we ran after the monkeys.'

'Never mind, I expect he'll be along in a minute,' said Granny.

Simon and Mary smiled at

each other. Then the doorbell
rang again.

'Well now, who can that be?'
said Granny.

The moment she opened the
door, in ran Jo-jo and So-so.

33

They were a bit wet from the rain but they were laughing and giggling as usual.

'It's the monkeys!' said Mary.

'What monkeys, my dear?' said Granny, peering closely at them through her glasses.

'The monkeys from the Zoo, Granny,' said Mary. 'They're called Jo-jo and So-so.'

'Hello, Jo-jo. Hello, So-so,' said Granny and she shook their hands. 'Now you all go into the sitting room and I'll make some tea.'

While Granny was making the tea Jo-jo and So-so explored the sitting room. They climbed all over the furniture, knocked a

plant pot off the window sill and
then they started swinging on
the curtains.

'Stop it! Stop it!' said Simon.

But they didn't take any
notice. Jo-jo was on one curtain
and So-so was on the other.
They swung backwards and
forwards, bumping in the
middle. Suddenly there was a
loud RRRrrrippp! and the
monkeys and curtains landed in
a heap on the floor. Granny
came in with the tea.

'That's it, make yourselves comfortable!' said Granny.

The tea was delicious. There was fruit cake and cream buns with lots of cream. Jo-jo squashed his bun so that the cream squirted all over So-so and then he drank his tea with loud slurping noises. Mary got hiccups.

When they had finished tea, Granny said, 'Let's play the piano!' and she went and opened the lid. Simon and Mary sat down beside her and they all started playing at once. Jo-jo ran up and down the keys and So-so did handstands on the lid, clapping with her feet.

Altogether it was the most awful
noise and quite loud enough to
be heard three miles away.

'What fun!' said Granny,
laughing.

Then somebody outside
started banging on the window.
It was Mrs Gloom from next
door. Granny opened the
window to hear what she was
saying.

'PLEASE WILL YOU STOP
THAT AWFUL NOISE!'
shouted Mrs Gloom. They
stopped playing but Mrs Gloom
went on shouting. 'I CAN'T
HEAR MYSELF THINK!'

'There's no need to shout,
dear,' said Granny.

Jo-jo and So-so saw that it
had stopped raining and ran out
through the open window.

'Good gracious! Monkeys!'
said Mrs Gloom, turning up her

nose. 'How disgusting!'

'Of course, dear,' said Granny.

'It's disgraceful!' said Mrs
Gloom. 'I shall telephone the
Zoo.' And she went back home
to do just that.

'Since it's stopped raining,'
said Granny to Simon and
Mary, 'why don't you go and

play with your friends in the
garden? They seem to be having
fun.' Jo-jo and So-so were
having a mud fight. Simon and
Mary grinned and ran outside.

It was the best mud fight ever.
There was lots of really squishy
mud after the rain. Simon and
Mary and Jo-jo and So-so threw
it at each other and fell over in
it and sat down in it. They got
absolutely covered in sloppy
squelchy brown mud.

Inside the house Granny was washing up the tea cups. The front doorbell rang. It was Mr Mullins from the Zoo. He was a bit out of breath and was holding a large butterfly net and a bunch of bananas. Mr Blaize, the Head Keeper, had been very cross that Jo-jo and So-so had escaped. He had gone red in the face and told Mr Mullins that if he didn't catch the monkeys straight away he was on crocodiles for a month. Mr Mullins did NOT want to look after the crocodiles.

'Hello,' said Mr Mullins to Granny. 'I'm from the Zoo. I understand there are some monkeys in your garden.'

'Are there?' said Granny. 'How exciting! We'd better go and see.'

Granny took Mr Mullins through the house to the garden.

'This is the garden,' said Granny.

There was a giggling squelchy squirmy mountain of mud in the middle of the garden. Four muddy faces grinned at them.

'There should be only two monkeys,' said Mr Mullins.

'But of course, dear,' said
Granny. 'The other two are my
grandchildren.'

'Oh yes,' said Mr Mullins, but
he wasn't at all sure which was
which. Better try the banana
trick, he thought and he waved
his bunch of bananas. Two of
the muddy figures ran towards
him.

Swooosh! Mr Mullins swept
down the butterfly net and
caught them.

'Got 'em!' he said. Funny
noises came from inside the net.
They sounded like cries for help.
'Just one of their tricks!' said Mr
Mullins and he carried the
bundle back to his van. 'Thank

you!' he called and he drove off.

'Well, my dears,' said Granny to the other two mud-covered figures who were giggling beside her. 'Perhaps you'd better have a bath now?' And she took them inside the house.

A short while later the front doorbell rang again. It was Simon and Mary's dad. He was out of breath, his clothes were all wet and he was holding two very soggy ice cream cones.

'Hello,' he gasped. 'Are Simon and Mary here?'

'Yes of course, dear,' said Granny. 'They're in the bath.'

'The little monkeys!' their dad exclaimed.

He ran up to the bathroom.
Funny noises were coming from
inside. He opened the door, then
dropped the soggy ice cream
cones and stared.

The bathroom was awash
with muddy water and there
were brown splashes on the
walls and the ceiling. Sitting in
the bath splashing and giggling
were two monkeys. Jo-jo and
So-so.

'Ohhh! Ohhh!' said Simon and Mary's dad as he ran back down the stairs. 'There are monkeys in the bathroom!'

'Of course, dear,' said Granny.

Mr Mullins was back at the Zoo. He had parked his van and was just taking the butterfly net bundle to the monkey cage when he met Mr Blaize, the Head Keeper.

'Ah, there you are, Mullins,' said Mr Blaize. 'So you got the monkeys all right, did you?'

'Yes, Sir. I've got the little monkeys here,' said Mr Mullins.

'Just a moment, Mullins,' said

Mr Blaize. There was a trail of dried mud from Mr Mullins' van. Mr Blaize looked at the butterfly net. He picked off a large piece of dried mud and blue cloth showed underneath.

'MULLINS!!' roared Mr Blaize, his face going purple. 'These aren't monkeys, they are children! You have captured somebody's children!'

Mr Mullins, shivering and stuttering, hastily put down the butterfly net. Simon and Mary struggled out.

'Are you all right?' asked Mr Blaize. Simon and Mary grinned.

'Yes, we're all right,' they said.

'I'm sorry. I'm so sorry!' said Mr Mullins.

'Now, Mullins,' said Mr Blaize. 'Go and get them an ice cream or something and then take them to see a few animals. Then you can all report to my office.'

'Yes, Mr Blaize,' said Mr Mullins who had gone pale.

'Please can we see the elephants?' said Simon.

'Yes, of course,' said Mr
Blaize. 'Make sure of it,
Mullins.'

'Mr Blaize! Mr Blaize!'
shouted Tony Nash, as he ran
towards them. 'The monkeys
have escaped again! And they're

feeding bananas to the
crocodiles!'

'MULLINS!' roared Mr
Blaize. But Mr Mullins didn't
answer.

He was lying on the ground
with his eyes closed.

Lucky Thunder

A book for Emily and Helen

I wish it would stop raining, Peter
thought as he watched the rain
drip off the leaves in the garden.
It had been raining for days and
Peter had had to stay indoors. To
make matters worse, his best
friend David was away on
holiday so he had no one to play
with.

Ding-dong, went the front
doorbell.

'Oh, who's that, at this time?' said Peter's mum. She sounded cross.

It was Miss Richards who lived in the flat upstairs. She had only moved in a couple of weeks before. Peter thought she looked a bit like a witch—a nice sort of witch, though. And she had a pet parrot called Thunder. Peter had heard it squawking.

'Hello, my darlings,' said Miss Richards. 'Sorry to trouble you, but Mother's in a fix and has asked if I can go and help her out. I was wondering if you'd mind looking after Thunder for me? Only till Saturday morning. I'd take him with me but Mother

can't stand the bird, poor dear.'

'Oh, Mum, please let's,' said
Peter. He liked the idea of having
a parrot to stay.

Mum looked rather doubtful.

'He's no trouble—really,' said
Miss Richards. 'No mess or
anything.'

'It's only till Saturday, Mum,'
said Peter. 'I'll look after him.'

'Oh, all right,' said Mum.

'Oh, thank you so much,' said Miss Richards. 'I'll go and fetch him.'

Thunder was a small green parrot. He sat quite still all through supper, looking very grumpy. He said nothing. He didn't even squawk.

'Miss Richards told me he could talk, Mum,' said Peter. 'He hasn't said a word.'

'I expect he's not in the mood,' said Mum. She got up and switched on the television for the weather forecast.

'I bet it's going to rain again,' said Peter gloomily.

'. . . And tomorrow there will be
more showers with longer
outbreaks of rain,' said the
weatherman.

'Squawk!' said Thunder,
suddenly waking up. 'Squawk.
Certainly not—sunny and hot!'

'He can talk, Mum,' said Peter. 'He can talk.'

'Well, let's hope he's right about the weather forecast,' said Peter's mum, smiling.

Thunder was right about the weather. Peter knew it the moment he opened his eyes. The sun was streaming in through the cracks in his bedroom curtains. He jumped out of bed and looked outside. There wasn't a cloud in the sky.

'Hello,' said Mum. 'Thunder's awake and enjoying his breakfast.'

'Squawk,' said Thunder, as Peter went into the kitchen.

'Hello, Thunder,' said Peter.

'Hello, hello,' said Thunder.

'What are you going to do today?' asked Mum.

'I'm going to be a pirate in search of treasure,' said Peter. 'With a real parrot.' That would be something to tell David, he thought.

'Well, don't dig up any of my vegetables,' said Mum.

Peter took Thunder out into the garden and started building his ship, the way he always did. He and David often played pirates. When he had finished, he put Thunder on board and they set off in search of treasure.

'Squawk,' said Thunder, happily. He liked the sunshine. He started preening.

Peter looked about with his telescope.

'Land ahoy!' he shouted. A desert island was in sight. The sea was a bit rough but they made it to the beach all right. Peter left Thunder to keep watch on board and went ashore to look for treasure.

'It must be here,' he said at last,
and started digging.

'Squawk,' said Thunder. 'Not
there, not there. Ten paces from
the tree under that cabbage.
Under the cabbage.'

Peter looked at the spot. It'll be all right if I just dig round the cabbage, he thought. So he started digging. Suddenly the cabbage fell over, uprooted.

'Peter! What are you doing?' said Mum, coming into the garden.

'But Mum . . .' began Peter.

'You naughty boy—it's ruined,' said Mum.

Peter stared sadly at the cabbage. Then something caught his eye.

'But Mum, look!' he said.

Quickly he dug in the soft earth
with his hands and pulled out a
small gold object. He rubbed off
the dirt and held it up.

'There is some treasure!' he
said.

'Goodness,' said Mum, staring.
'It's my locket. I lost it ages ago.'
She was smiling, the cabbage
forgotten. 'I wonder how it got
there.'

'Thunder told me where to
look,' said Peter.

'Well done, Thunder!' said
Mum.

'Squawk,' said Thunder.

Grandad came round for supper. Peter told him all about the treasure and how Thunder had helped him find it.

'Fancy that,' said Grandad, looking at Thunder. 'Clever bird. Who'd have thought it?'

Mum had bought some cream cakes to celebrate. She was very pleased to have her locket back.

'We could all go to the fête tomorrow if the weather's nice,' said Grandad.

'I wonder what the weather forecast is,' said Mum.

'Thunder and lightning!' said Thunder.

The next day was Saturday. Despite what Thunder had said, it was a sunny day again. If anything, it was hotter than the day before.

Miss Richards called in the morning to collect Thunder. Peter was sorry to see him go.

'I really enjoyed having him,' he said.

'Well, he seems to have enjoyed his stay,' said Miss Richards.

Peter told her about finding his mum's locket. 'Thunder told me where to look,' he said.

'Did he now?' said Miss Richards. 'What a clever bird.' She looked at him admiringly. 'Are you coming to the fête this afternoon?' she asked Peter.

'Yes, I think so,' said Peter.

'Well, I shall be there, telling fortunes. I'll do yours for free if you like. Just look for my tent.'

'Thank you,' said Peter.

'Bye for now, then, my darlings!' said Miss Richards and she disappeared upstairs with Thunder.

In the afternoon Grandad brought his car round so that

they could all go to the fête.

'Lovely day again,' he said.

The fête was in the grounds of Rington School. Coloured bunting hung from the trees and there were lots of stalls, piled with jumble and home made jam, craftwork and cakes. The Mayor of Rington was there to open the fête and to do the Prize Draw.

'Here,' said Grandad to Peter,
'buy yourself something with
this.' And he slipped a pound coin
into Peter's hand.

'Thanks, Grandad,' said Peter.
He went to look for something to
spend it on. Mum was looking at
stuff on a jumble stall. She picked
up some bookends with horses on.
Mum liked horses. Grandad
started looking at some old books.
Peter had just decided to buy a
fishing rod when he noticed a tent

nearby with a notice outside. It
said:

FORTUNE TELLER
Madame Richards will read
your fortune for £1

That must be our Miss Richards
from the flat upstairs, Peter
thought. Then he heard a squawk
from inside the tent. She must
have Thunder with her. Peter
pulled at Grandad's sleeve.

'Grandad,' he said. 'Can I go and have my fortune told? Miss Richards said she'd do it for free.' He wanted to see Thunder again.

'For free, did she?' said Grandad. 'Well, all right. I'll wait outside.'

Peter went into the tent. It was dark and mysterious inside. It took a moment for Peter's eyes to

get used to the darkness. Miss
Richards was sitting at a small
table. He couldn't see Thunder.

'Hello, my darling, come on in,'
said Miss Richards.

'Squawk,' said Thunder. 'Hello,
hello, hello.'

'So he is here!' said Peter. He
saw Thunder behind Miss
Richards.

'Why, yes,' said Miss Richards.
'Thunder's my lucky charm. He
helps me a lot, you know.'

'Like he helped me with the
buried treasure?' said Peter.

'Yes, that's it. Lucky Thunder,
he is,' said Miss Richards. 'Now
then, sit very still and I'll look
into my crystal ball.'

Peter sat and watched Miss
Richards. She peered into a large
crystal ball on the table, waving
her hands around it. She
muttered strange words to
herself. Thunder sat behind her
on his perch. He had a funny far-
away look in his eyes, as though
he was day-dreaming.

'Ah,' said Miss Richards. 'The

mists begin to clear . . . I see a boy in a red T-shirt . . .'

'I've got a red T-shirt—that must be me,' said Peter.

'It is sunny, very bright sunshine,' continued Miss Richards. 'You are holding a spade and you are smiling . . . There is your mother and she is also smiling.'

Suddenly, Thunder seemed to wake with a start. 'Squawk! Squawk!' he said.

'Oh, the picture's fading,' murmured Miss Richards. 'Thunder, you funny thing, what is it?'

Thunder was shuffling about on his perch, flapping his wings. Suddenly he squawked loudly.

'Four five six, just the ticket! Four five six, just the ticket!' he said.

'Whatever do you mean, Thunder?' said Miss Richards.

Thunder went quiet again. He had lost the far-away look.

'I'm afraid the crystal has gone cloudy,' said Miss Richards. 'So that's all I can tell you. But it looks as though you'll be getting nice weather, anyway.'

'Thunder and lightning,' said
Thunder. 'Thunder and
lightning.'

'Oh, take no notice,' said Miss
Richards. 'He's always saying
that. Well, see you later, my
darling.'

'Thank you very much,' said Peter politely and he ran out into the sun. Grandad and Mum were waiting. The sun seemed very hot and bright after the tent.

'Well, what's going to happen?' asked Grandad.

'The weather's going to be all right,' said Peter.

'Is that all?' said Grandad. 'Well, we could do with more days like today.'

A man with a microphone started making an announcement. 'Ladies and Gentlemen. Your attention please. At three o'clock the Rington Drum Majorettes will give a display. Then, after that, The great Mundini will escape from a trunk padlocked thirty-three times. And don't forget, the Mayor will draw the raffle at four o'clock! First prize a holiday in Spain. Tickets are still on sale over here.'

'Coo, a holiday in Spain,' said Mum. 'That would be nice!'

'Have a go, then,' said Grandad.

'Oh, I never win that sort of thing,' said Mum.

'Go on,' said Grandad. 'I'll buy you a ticket.'

They walked over to where a man was selling raffle tickets. Peter looked at the prizes. There were some photos of Spain, showing where the first prize winners went for their holiday. The other prizes were quite good as well. There was an enormous picnic hamper full of food, there was a kitchen food mixer and there was a box of wine. Grandad

bought some tickets. Peter could
hear Thunder squawking nearby
and it reminded him of
something. He looked in his
pocket for his money. Grandad
and Mum were about to wander
off elsewhere.

'Wait, Mum. I want one,' said
Peter.

'But Peter, are you sure?' said Mum.

'Yes,' said Peter. His mind was made up.

He went up to the man selling the tickets.

'Have you still got number four five six? he asked.

'Well, let's see,' said the man. 'Yes. Fancy that, look—the next in the book.'

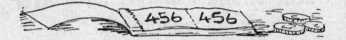

The man tore out the ticket and gave it to Peter. Peter handed over his money. He stared at the ticket for a moment and then put it away safely in his pocket.

The Rington Drum Majorettes did their display. They sometimes got a bit out of step but it was fun to watch and everybody clapped loudly when they finished. Then

the Great Mundini appeared. He was tied hand and foot and then put into a large trunk. Great chains and padlocks were put round the trunk. Peter couldn't think how he would ever escape from all that. An assistant put up a screen so you couldn't see what was happening and then there was a drum roll. Suddenly there was a crash as the screen wobbled and fell over. Everybody could see the Great Mundini wriggling out of a hole in the bottom of the trunk. They all roared with laughter. Poor Mr Mundini went red all over and disappeared back into his tent as quickly as he could.

'Ha, well that's that. How about a cup of tea?' said Grandad. He was very fond of tea.

'That would be nice,' said Mum.

Tea and orange juice was being served at the other end of the fête. There were strawberry tarts made with fresh strawberries.

'They look good,' said Grandad and he bought some for them all. Peter ate his very quickly.

'Oh, look,' said Mum. I think
the Mayor is going to do the Prize
Draw.'

The Mayor had got up on the
platform.

'Ladies and Gentlemen,' said
the man with the microphone.
'The Mayor will now draw the
winning tickets for the Grand
Prize Draw.'

There was a large drum with all the tickets inside. The man who had made the announcement turned a handle and the drum went round and round. When it stopped he lifted a flap at the top. The Mayor put his hand inside and pulled out a ticket.

'First prize,' said the Mayor into the microphone. 'First prize is blue ticket number four hundred and fifty-six.'

Peter stared at the ticket in his hand. Four five six.

'Good gracious, Peter's won!' said Grandad.

'What?' said Mum, disbelieving.

'Peter's got the winning ticket,' said Grandad. 'Come on!'

Peter got shakily to his feet. He walked unsteadily with Mum and Grandad up to the platform. The Mayor smiled an enormous smile at him.

'The winner,' said the Mayor. 'Jolly good!' and he shook Peter's hand. 'What's your name?'

'Peter,' said Peter.

'Well, Peter, you've won a

holiday in Spain. Well done!' said
the Mayor.

Peter didn't know what to say.
He still couldn't believe it. Then
he heard a squawk. There was
Miss Richards with Thunder.

'Squawk,' said Thunder. 'Just
the ticket! Happy holidays!
Happy holidays!' and he flapped
his wings.

As they walked back to the car,
dark clouds were gathering
overhead. There was the rumble
of distant thunder and the first
few spots of rain fell on the
pavement.

Lucky Thunder! thought Peter.